MW00877776

THE CHRISTMAS THINGAMAJIG

by
LYNN MANUEL

Illustrated by
CAROL BENIOFF

DUTTON CHILDREN'S BOOKS · NEW YORK

CIP Data is available.

Published in the United States 2002 by Dutton Children's Books,
a division of Penguin Putnam Books for Young Readers
345 Hudson Street, New York, New York 10014
www.penguinputnam.com

Designed by Alyssa Morris
Printed in Hong Kong
First Edition
ISBN 0-525-46120-5
1 3 5 7 9 10 8 6 4 2

To Patricia Mary, my sister
L.M.

For my grandmothers, Mimi and Nana—two headstrong,
independent women who cheered, teased, and prodded me
along my way
C.B.

Outside the frosty car windows, the moonlit fields of snow rushed by in the night. The same as always.

Chloe wondered how things could look the same and yet feel so different.

"Why couldn't we just stay at home for Christmas?" she asked.

"We've discussed this already, Chloe," her mother answered. "Grandpa needs us."

"Besides," her father added, "you know that coming out here is a tradition."

Chloe sighed. Nobody seemed to understand. Christmas would never be the same again. Not without the wisps of silver hair floating around Grandma's face, and the sound of her singsongy voice calling them to breakfast, and the soapy-clean smell of her hugs.

And not without Grandma's thingamajigs.

Why did Grandma have to die? Chloe squeezed her eyes shut and tried not to think about how things used to be. It hurt too much.

When the car pulled into the long driveway, she opened her eyes to see Grandpa standing there, all alone in the square of yellow light from the opened door.

"Good to see you, Chloe!" he said as he wrapped his arms around her.

"Good to see you, too, Grandpa," she answered.

For an instant she looked up into his eyes, but she saw the emptiness there and quickly looked away.

The house looked the same as always with its puffy chairs and its wallpaper of faded roses. But it didn't feel the same. It felt like a museum house Chloe had visited once, with roped-off rooms. A house where nobody really lived anymore. It was just for people to poke around in and peek at and see what it used to be like once upon a time.

While they sat around the kitchen table, Grandpa put water on to boil in the kettle and brought Grandma's teacups down. The old teacups. The ones missing their matching saucers.

Out of the corner of her eye, Chloe could see the Christmas tree decorations piled neatly on a chair by the door. She knew there was a shoebox in that pile. And on the shoebox were the words "Christmas Thingamajigs" in Grandma's fancy handwriting, the "i"s dotted with circles like little moons.

As the voices murmured at the table, Chloe sat very still. She didn't turn her head to look at the box of thingamajigs. That was one of her tricks—looking out of the corners of her eyes, standing far back, and squinting. Tricks so that she would never really have to look at the things that hurt.

But no matter how hard she tried, Chloe couldn't keep the memories away.

Every year after decorating the tree, she would stand back and say, "Hmmm, this tree still needs a little something."

And Grandma would laugh. "Well, it just so happens that I have a little something." Then with a twirl and a big "Ta-da!" Grandma would hold up a thingamajig made from a little of this and a little of that—a toy soldier fashioned from empty spools or a dimpled dough bear or a pinecone owl. She always said she never knew what it would turn out to be. She just made it up as she went along.

It was a tradition, just like Chloe and Grandma dancing all around the Christmas tree.

Later that night, when she was curled up in the old bed that sagged in the middle, there was a tap-tap-tap at the door, and Grandpa stuck his head in the room.

"Need anything, Chloe?" he asked. "More blankets, maybe?"

"No, thanks."

"You sure?"

"Don't worry, Grandpa. I'll be fine."

"Good."

Then the door clicked shut.

Those were the same words Grandma had used that day in the hospital. "Don't worry. I'll be fine."

Chloe had wanted to believe her, but the brightness had gone from Grandma's eyes, and Chloe was afraid to look at her. She had backed farther and farther away from Grandma until she was just too far away to look at her anymore.

As Chloe drifted off to sleep, she remembered the sound of Grandma's soft-soled slippers on the stairs, and she wished that time would turn back. But deep inside, she knew it wouldn't.

The next few days passed much the same as they did every year. Chloe went tobogganing down the snowy slopes and skated on the icy pond. But after supper, she went upstairs and stayed there all alone, except for Maxie, the old brown cat. Sometimes she read. And sometimes she just listened to the wind whistling through the eaves.

Then one evening, her mother came looking for her.

"You know you always get the Christmas tree with Grandpa," her mother said when Chloe wrinkled up her face. "I used to go Christmas tree hunting with Grandpa, too, when I was your age. I always thought there was something special about going at night when the stars were out. And I remember how..."

Chloe could hear a sudden quiver in her mother's voice.

"...your grandma always had hot chocolate waiting for us. It's kind of a tradition."

So that was that.

The branches hissed over the snow as Chloe and Grandpa pulled the tree behind them on the toboggan. Grandpa was wearing his Christmas-tree-hunting hat—the green one with the earflaps. The same one as always.

He peered into the night sky from under the brim. "It was a night like this when I first held your grandma's hand," he said. Then a grin crept over his face. "Did I ever tell you how we met?"

Chloe looked away without answering. She didn't want to talk about Grandma.

Halfway up a soft slope, Grandpa stopped to rest his tired leg. The one that made him limp.

"She was working in a fish market," he said, rubbing the small of his back. "I went in there one day to buy some halibut for my supper. That was the first time I ever laid eyes on your grandma."

Chloe looked at the tiny balls of snow that clung to her mittens, then at the creek that wiggled its way through the darkness, and finally at the smoke that swirled out from the chimney in the distance. She looked everywhere except at Grandpa.

"I couldn't work up the nerve to ask her out, though," Grandpa
was saying. "Just kept going back for more halibut. Ate so much, it
was nearly coming out of my ears! Then one day I was unwrapping
my bit of fish, and I noticed something penciled in a corner of the
brown butcher paper."

"What was it?" Chloe asked the question before she could stop
herself.

"Little hearts," said Grandpa. He shook his head as if he still found
it hard to believe. "Imagine her drawing little hearts on brown
butcher paper just for me!"

For a few minutes, they were silent. As they started up the slope again, Chloe spoke her thoughts aloud.

"Grandpa, doesn't it make you sad? To think about Grandma, I mean."

When he answered, his words came out all cracked. "Sure, it makes me sad. But you know something, Chloe? Thinking about Grandma makes me feel good, too. Grandma had a word for it."

"She did?"

Grandpa nodded. "'Bittersweet.' That's what memories can be sometimes."

When they got back to the house, Chloe sat by the fire, sipping hot chocolate and twisting the tassels of a cushion this way and that, while her father helped Grandpa set the tree up in its stand and her mother gave directions of a smidgen to the left and a tad to the right. The same as always.

The room was filled with the spicy scent of pine, but Chloe
caught the faintest whiff of something else. She lifted the cushion
and sniffed at the blue fabric. It smelled of something pleasant and
familiar.

It smelled of Grandma.

She hugged the cushion hard as something inside her seemed to
crumble. As tears sprang to her eyes, she wiped them away and
threw the cushion to the floor.

"It's not the same!" she cried. "And I don't want to do things the same!"
When she saw the look of surprise on their faces, she turned and ran
from the room.

For what seemed like an eternity, she lay in the sag of the old bed with her eyes closed. Then Grandpa came up with milk and some toast with apple-cider marmalade.

He kneeled beside her bed.

"She was as smart as a whip, that grandma of yours!"

He spoke so suddenly, it made Chloe jump.

"Never told anybody this before," he said, "but I didn't know how to read until your grandma taught me. Back when we were first married. Your grandma was like that. Always helping me face new things."

Chloe looked over in surprise. She didn't know what to say, so she didn't say anything at all.

"Life can be scary sometimes," he added in a whisper.

"You get scared, Grandpa?"

"Scared stiff, now and again," he said. "Never did have any family until Grandma came along. Now I feel like one of her old teacups without its matching saucer."

The floorboards creaked as Grandpa got up and walked over to the window. "Life is full of changes. Guess I need to know there are some things I can count on. Some things that'll never change."

"Like what?"

"Like traditions," said Grandpa. "You know, carved pumpkins on Halloween. Painted eggs at Easter. Housecleaning in the spring." He was quiet for a moment, then he added, "Traditions help me face the new things...the things I have to make up as I go along."

Chloe opened her mouth to speak, then closed it again.

There was something she needed to say, but the words wouldn't
come. Finally, she just blurted them out.

"Before Grandma died...I didn't want to visit her in the hospital."

"I know."

Chloe choked back a sob. "I didn't want to see her anymore,
Grandpa! She was just lying there in that bed. I couldn't look at her
like that. It hurt too much!"

For a long moment, her words seemed to hang in the air between
them.

Then Grandpa said softly, "Grandma knew you loved her, Chloe."
Moving closer, he reached out in the darkness and placed something
in her hands. "She wanted you to have this. Said it might keep your
heart from feeling so heavy."

On his way out of the room, Grandpa turned. "We all handle pain
in our own way," he said. "And in our own time."

When the door clicked shut, Chloe turned on the light beside the
bed and looked down at the box she was holding. Penciled in a
corner were little hearts.

She lifted the lid and found a Christmas thingamajig inside, made from bits of wool and scraps of clothing. Pipe cleaners were twisted together so that the two figures seemed to be holding hands. And the legs were bent as if they were dancing.

Chloe grinned, even as a tear slipped down her cheek, and she remembered the little things about Grandma. The funny little things. The purple jacket unbuttoned at the bottom to make room for Grandma's roly-poly hips. The big straw garden hat unraveling at the brim. The pom-poms bobbing up and down on her slippered feet as she danced with Chloe around and around the Christmas tree.

When the house was quiet, Chloe tiptoed down the stairs, and in the soft glow of the moonlight shining through the window, she hung Grandma's thingamajig on the Christmas tree.

When she turned, she saw Grandpa standing in the light from the doorway.

"I miss Grandma," she said.

"So do I, Chloe."

With a sudden thought, she added, "Can you dance, Grandpa?"

He laughed softly. "Well, I've been known to kick up my heels from time to time," he said. "Might be the two of us could do a bit of a jig."

Chloe thought for a moment.

"A thingama-jig!" Then with a twirl and a big "Ta-da!" she said, "We could do a thingama-jig, Grandpa!"

They smiled at each other and began to dance around and around in the moonlight, with a little dip here and a little twirl there. Just making it up as they went along.

Q
1.03